Crumble and Custard

Crumble and Custard looked at each other. Did that mean what they thought it meant?

"OK," Oliver agreed, picking up a pen. "I'll bring the pups with me. If you could just give me the address . . ."

"Yippee!" woofed Custard. "We're going with Oliver to cook party food! That's *much* better than going to the park!"

Titles in Jenny Dale's PUPPY TALES™ series

1. Gus the Greedy Puppy
2. Lily the Lost Puppy
3. Spot the Sporty Puppy
4. Lenny the Lazy Puppy
5. Max the Mucky Puppy
6. Billy the Brave Puppy
7. Nipper the Noisy Puppy
8. Tilly the Tidy Puppy
9. Spike the Special Puppy
10. Hattie the Homeless Puppy
11. Merlin the Magic Puppy
12. Fergus the Friendly Puppy
13. Snowy the Surprise Puppy
14. Bubble and Squeak
15. Crumble and Custard

All of Jenny Dale's PUPPY TALES books can be ordered at your local bookshop or are available by post from Book Service by Post (tel: 01624 675137)

Crumble and Custard

by Jenny Dale

Illustrated by Susan Hellard

A Working Partners Book

MACMILLAN CHILDREN'S BOOKS

Special thanks to Narinder Dhami

First published 2001 by Macmillan Children's Books
a division of Macmillan Publishers Limited
25 Eccleston Place, London SW1W 9NF
Basingstoke and Oxford
www.macmillan.com

Associated companies throughout the world

Created by Working Partners Limited
London W6 0QT

ISBN 0 330 48424 9

7 9 8 6

A CIP catalogue record for this book is available from
the British Library.

Typeset by SX Composing DTP, Rayleigh, Essex
Printed and bound in Great Britain by Mackays of Chatham plc, Kent

Chapter One

"Is Oliver coming yet?" Crumble whined. The Labrador puppy was trying to climb up onto the sofa. He was using his brother Custard as a stepping stone.

"Get your paw out of my ear, Crumble!" Custard woofed crossly.

"Help me get onto the sofa, then," Crumble panted, trying to heave himself up. "I want to climb onto the window ledge and look for Oliver."

"What's going on here?" a voice barked suddenly.

Crumble was so surprised, he let go of the sofa and tumbled onto the floor. Luckily, Custard broke his fall.

"What *are* you doing?" yapped Lady the spaniel, padding into the room.

"I was trying to climb up onto the sofa to see if Oliver was coming," Crumble woofed.

"You *know* you're not allowed on the sofa," Lady replied sternly. "You're a bad boy, Crumble!"

Custard barked, giving his brother a teasing nip on the tail. Next moment they were rolling around on the carpet, play-fighting.

"What are you two up to?" said Mrs James, popping her head round the door. Crumble and Custard belonged to Mrs James's son, Oliver. But while he was at work they stayed with Mrs James and her old spaniel, Lady.

"Nothing, Granny James!" Crumble and Custard barked together, putting on their best "cute" faces. Suddenly the ears of both puppies pricked up.

"I can hear a motorbike!" Crumble woofed excitedly.

"It's Oliver," Custard barked.

"And I heard it first!"

"No, *I* did," Crumble yapped.

Still arguing, the two pups rushed to the front door.

A moment later, Oliver came in. Custard and Crumble went mad, jumping around his feet and barking loudly.

"Hello, boys!" said Oliver,

grinning. He took off his crash helmet and ran a hand through his fair hair. Then he scooped the pups up, one in each arm. "Have you been good today?"

"*I* have," Crumble yapped, licking his owner's cheek. "But Custard ran off with Lady's biscuit!"

"Ooh, I did not!" Custard woofed back, nibbling Oliver's ear. "Anyway, Granny James told Crumble off for chewing the rug!"

"What have you been cooking today, Oliver?" Crumble pushed his nose into Oliver's neck. Their owner was a chef, so he always smelled *delicious*. In fact, biscuit-coloured Crumble and pale yellow Custard were named after

Oliver's favourite pudding.

The pups knew that Oliver went to people's houses to cook food for them when they were having special parties. Crumble and Custard always thought it was *most* unfair that they weren't allowed to go along too.

"Hi, Mum," Oliver said. "Thanks for looking after the Terrible Two."

"It's a pleasure – sort of," his mum laughed. "Now, you three, enjoy your weekend."

"We will," Oliver promised.

Crumble and Custard looked at each other in delight. So tomorrow was the weekend! That meant Oliver wouldn't leave them and go to work. He'd stay at home and play!

"Brilliant!" the two pups barked, their tails wagging happily.

"Bye, Mum," Oliver called as he carried Crumble and Custard over to his motorbike. "You have a good weekend too, and give my love to Gran."

"Lady and I will be back from Gran's on Sunday night," his mum replied. "So I'll be here to look after the pups as usual on Monday morning."

Oliver's motorbike had a sidecar which Crumble and Custard could ride in. They loved it. The sidecar had a cover attached, which meant that they were quite safe. It was clear, so that they could look out too.

"OK, boys, let's go," Oliver said, popping the pups into the sidecar and closing it carefully.

"A whole weekend with Oliver," Crumble yapped happily as their owner revved up the motorbike engine.

"Fantastic!" Custard agreed.

*

At first, the weekend went just as Crumble and Custard had hoped.

On Saturday morning they all had a lie-in. The puppies curled up in their favourite place next to Oliver. Then they all went down to the kitchen. First, Oliver fed Crumble and Custard their puppy food, then he got out the pancake pan to make his own breakfast.

Crumble, who always finished eating first, snuffled around Oliver's feet as he began to mix the pancake batter. "Yum!" he yapped. "Leave a bit of room for some pancake, Custard!"

"Don't worry, I will!" Custard snuffled back, as he finished off his puppy biscuits.

Just then the phone rang. Oliver

went into the hall to answer it. The puppies rushed after him.

"Go away!" Crumble barked crossly as Oliver picked up the phone. "Oliver's making pancakes."

"Yes, and you're not having any, whoever you are." Custard added.

"Quiet, boys," Oliver said sternly. "Hello?"

"Maybe we should guard the pancake mix," Custard growled. "Someone might come and steal it."

"Good idea," Crumble agreed.

The two pups trotted back to the kitchen.

"You're having an important lunch party today, and you want

me to come and cook for you?"
Oliver was saying.

Crumble and Custard skidded
to a halt outside the kitchen door
when they heard *that*. Their tails
stopped wagging. Oliver was
going to *work* today? What about
their lovely weekend?

"Well, I can see it's an
emergency, Mrs Gill," Oliver said.
"But I can't, I'm afraid."

The pups' tails began to wag
again, just a little.

"I've got no one to look after my
two puppies," Oliver went on.
"They usually stay with my mum
while I'm working, but she's
away for the weekend. And I
can't leave them on their own
because they destroy things."

11

"That's because *you* chewed one of Oliver's wooden spoons, Crumble!" Custard yapped.

"Well, *you* ate half his rubber plant!" Crumble argued.

"I suppose I could . . ." Oliver was saying. "But only if there's somewhere safe for them to play while I'm working."

Crumble and Custard looked at each other. Did that mean what they thought it meant?

"OK," Oliver agreed, picking up a pen. "I'll bring the pups with me then. If you could just give me the address . . ."

"YES!" Crumble barked excitedly, running round in circles to celebrate. "Oliver's taking us with him."

"Yippee!" woofed Custard. "We're going with Oliver to cook party food. That's *much* better than going to the park!"

"Yes," Crumble agreed. "It's even better than a bit of pancake after breakfast!"

Chapter Two

"OK, boys, we're here." Oliver turned off the motorbike engine. "Look at this posh house!"

"It's huge!" Crumble gasped.

"Does the Queen live here?" asked Custard.

The Gills' house was at the end of a winding driveway. It had a large garden with a waterfall and lots of statues. Crumble and Custard could hardly wait to dive out of the sidecar and explore.

"Now listen, you two," Oliver said sternly. "I want you to be on your best behaviour. Is that clear?"

"Yes, Oliver," the pups woofed.

Oliver clipped their leads onto their collars, and let them out. He led them over to the front door. But before he had a chance to ring the bell, the door flew open.

A tall woman with black hair stood there, beaming at them. "Hello, I'm Mrs Gill," she said. "Thank goodness you could help me out, Oliver. And aren't your dogs gorgeous!"

Crumble and Custard liked Mrs Gill already. They snuffled at her fingers as she gave them both a quick pat.

"Come in," said Mrs Gill. She hurried them across a beautiful hallway with thick rugs and a sweeping staircase, then into a huge kitchen. "Like I told you on the phone, my usual chef has flu, and you can see what a mess we're in."

Crumble and Custard's eyes nearly popped out of their heads. They'd never *seen* so much food! There were containers and packets on all the worktops, as well as bags and boxes of colourful fruit and vegetables.

"*How* many guests did you say

were coming to the party, Mrs Gill?" Oliver asked, looking just as dazed as the puppies.

"Oh, only twenty," Mrs Gill replied. "But my daughter Yasmin is having a birthday party in two days' time. That's why there's so much food." She waved a hand around the kitchen. "Use whatever you like. There's a joint of beef for the main course, but the starters and pudding are up to you."

"OK," Oliver agreed.

"The guests will be arriving at about two o'clock," Mrs Gill went on. "Come and see the dining room." She led them all out of the kitchen and into the big room next door.

It had a long wooden table that was laid with sparkling plates and cutlery, and huge bowls of flowers. Two large French windows stood open at the far end of the room, leading out into the garden.

Crumble and Custard both sniffed the air, their black noses twitching. There were loads of exciting new smells to explore!

A man wearing shorts and a T-shirt hurried from the garden, into the room.

"This is my husband," said Mrs Gill. "Darling, say hello to Oliver, our new chef."

Smiling, Mr Gill came across the room. "Thanks for coming to our rescue like this," he began. Then he spotted Crumble and Custard, and stopped in his tracks. "Oh no! Keep those dogs away from me!"

"Don't worry," Oliver said quickly, "they're very friendly."

"Oh, no, it's not that," Mr Gill muttered. He began to sneeze loudly. "*A-tishoo*!"

"Oh, I forgot about your allergy!" said Mrs Gill. "You'd better go upstairs, darling."

Still sneezing, Mr Gill hurried over to the door, keeping as far away from the two puppies as he could.

"What's the matter with *him*?" Crumble asked. Mr Gill hadn't even given them a pat.

"Maybe he's got a cold," Custard suggested. "Remember

when Oliver had one? He kept sneezing all the time."

"The puppies should be quite safe in the garden," Mrs Gill went on. "My daughter Yasmin's out there somewhere. She'll love them."

Oliver nodded. "I'll just get them settled, and then I'll start work."

"Super," said Mrs Gill. "Oh, excuse me." And she dashed off to answer the phone.

"Come on, Oliver," Crumble and Custard woofed together. They began to drag him towards the garden. "Let's go and explore."

Chapter Three

"*Please* let us off our leads, Oliver!" Crumble snuffled, as they walked through the enormous garden.

"Grr!" Custard grabbed his lead between his teeth and shook it crossly from side to side. "Let me go, Oliver!"

"Stop it, you two," Oliver scolded, unclipping their leads as they walked across the lawn. "I just wanted to check that there's no way for you to get out of the garden."

"Look, Custard." Crumble had spotted something interesting.

"Where?" Custard woofed.

"There!" Crumble barked impatiently. "That must be Yasmin."

A girl with long black hair was lying on the grass ahead of them. She was reading a book.

Her eyes lit up at the sight of the two puppies. "Hi, I'm Yasmin," she called to Oliver. "Are you the chef?"

"Yeah, I'm Oliver, and this is

Crumble and Custard," Oliver
replied.

"I'm Crumble," Crumble
panted. "Stroke me first!"

"I'm Custard," Custard yapped.
"Stroke *me* first!"

Yasmin laughed. She bent down
and put an arm round each
puppy. "They're so cute," she

cried. "Do you want me to look after them while you're working?"

"Oh, thanks!" Oliver said gratefully. "Sure you don't mind?"

Yasmin shook her head. "No, I love dogs."

"Great!" Crumble and Custard barked together.

"You two behave yourselves, then," Oliver said. He scratched the puppies' heads affectionately and handed their leads to Yasmin. "See you later."

"Look at me, Yasmin," Crumble woofed as Oliver hurried off. "I can roll over!" And he lay on the grass and rolled about, showing his fat tummy.

"No, look at me, Yasmin," Custard boasted. "I can catch my tail!" And he started running round in circles.

Yasmin grinned. "You're both lovely!" she said, kissing the tops of their heads.

Crumble and Custard had a brilliant time. They played Chase-the-Twig and Hide-and-Seek. And whenever the pups got out of breath, Yasmin picked them up and gave them lots of cuddles.

"Let's go inside and have a drink," Yasmin suggested as they all lay panting on the grass after playing Tag. "And we can see how Oliver's getting on too."

As they got near the house, Crumble and Custard's noses

began to twitch like mad. There were some *delicious* smells coming from the kitchen. They both began to feel very hungry as well as thirsty.

Oliver was spooning crumble over some apples in a large dish. His face was red because the kitchen was hot. But apart from that, he looked very calm and organised.

"I'm just going to get some water for the puppies, Oliver," Yasmin told him.

Oliver smiled at her. "Thanks," he said.

He grinned at Crumble and Custard. "Have you been good, boys?"

"*Course* we have," Crumble

yapped proudly.

"Everything smells great, Oliver," Yasmin said shyly. She filled a bowl from the cold tap, then put it down on the floor. "How are you getting on?" she asked, as Crumble and Custard lapped at their water.

"Well, I've made the starters, and they're already in the dining room," Oliver said. "And I'm just finishing the pud. Then I'll put the beef in the oven. All I have to do then is chop the veggies and make salads."

"I can't wait to try it all," Yasmin grinned. Then she frowned as the sound of a car came through the open window. "I wonder who that is?"

"Well, as long as it's not the guests," Oliver laughed.

Yasmin went out into the hallway to have a look, and the puppies trotted after her.

"Wheeee!" Custard barked as he skidded on the polished floor. "This is fun, Crumble!"

Crumble tried to run after his brother, and slid along the floor too. "Let's see how far we can slide!" he yapped.

Yasmin stared out of the hall window. A big car was pulling up outside the house, and another was just turning in through the gates. "Oh no!" she cried. "It *is* the guests – and it's only twelve o'clock! They're two hours early!"

Chapter Four

Crumble and Custard scrambled to a halt, mid-slide.

"The guests are here?" Crumble woofed. "They *can't* be."

"Go away," Custard growled. "Oliver's not ready yet."

Yasmin grabbed the pups and dashed back to the kitchen.

"Oliver!" she gasped. "The guests *are* here!"

"What?" Oliver was pouring custard into a jug. He was so surprised, he dripped some on the floor.

"Oh, yum," yapped Crumble and Custard, clambering out of Yasmin's arms to clean it up.

"See how helpful we are?" snuffled Crumble.

"What are we going to do?" Yasmin wailed. "Mum and Dad must have told them the wrong time."

Oliver looked at the large joint of beef. "Oh, no," he groaned. "The beef will never be ready in time. It will take hours to cook."

"Don't worry, Oliver," Crumble barked. "If we don't open the door, they'll all go away!"

"I'd better go and tell Mum and Dad," Yasmin said. She raced upstairs with the puppies at her heels. "Mum!" she yelled, running into her parents' bedroom. "The guests are here!"

"What!" Mrs Gill rushed out of

the bathroom. She was wearing her dressing gown, and she had a creamy facepack all over her face.

"Help!" Crumble barked. "Mrs Gill's face has turned green!"

"I'm scared," Custard whined, and tried to crawl under the bed.

"I don't believe it," Mrs Gill cried. "Will Oliver be able to serve lunch early?"

Yasmin shook her head. "He said that the beef isn't even in yet, and it will take hours to cook."

Just then the doorbell rang. Mrs Gill groaned.

"Who's that at the door?" Mr Gill came into the bedroom.

"It's the guests, Dad," Yasmin said urgently. "They're early."

"What?" Her dad glanced down

at his shorts and T-shirt. "But I'm not even dressed yet – *a-tishoo*! Will somebody please take those dogs downstairs!"

"Show the guests into the sitting room, Yasmin," Mrs Gill said. She wiped her face with a tissue. "Offer them drinks and tell them we'll be down as soon as we can. Then tell Oliver to put the beef in the freezer and use the chicken drumsticks out of the fridge. They'll cook much more quickly. We can buy some more tomorrow for your birthday party."

Yasmin nodded and dashed downstairs again with the puppies right behind her.

"Mum and Dad are getting changed," she told Oliver

breathlessly. "I've got to let the guests in and give them drinks. Oh – and forget the beef – do chicken drumsticks instead – they're in the fridge!" she called.

The doorbell rang again.

"OK, leave the pups here with me," said Oliver. He was looking *very* red in the face now.

Yasmin rushed out, shutting the kitchen door behind her.

Crumble and Custard crept quietly under the kitchen table, and sat cuddled close together.

"Poor Oliver," Crumble whined. "Will he get into trouble?"

"I don't know," Custard whimpered.

After a while, Yasmin came back. "Can I do anything to help,

Oliver?" she asked.

Oliver nodded gratefully. "Put my crumble and custard in the dining room out of the way, will you?" Then he went into the pantry to fetch some potatoes.

"OK," Yasmin said. She picked up the pups and took them out of the kitchen.

"Don't *want* to go in the dining room," Crumble yapped.

"We want to stay with you," Custard snuffled.

"Now be good," Yasmin warned them as she put them in the dining room. And she shut the door quickly.

Crumble and Custard looked glum. But then, at exactly the same moment, their noses began to twitch.

"I smell food!" Crumble woofed excitedly.

"And it's close by!" Custard added.

Both pups bounded over to the big table, tails wagging.

"It must be up there!" Custard yapped. "Perhaps it's our lunch. That's why Oliver told Yasmin to put us in here."

"But how are we going to reach it?" Crumble woofed.

"Easy!" Custard yapped back. He began to climb up the nearest chair, using the bar to help him. It was a bit of a struggle, but he made it onto the seat. From there, he could just about get onto the top of the table.

"Hey, wait for me!" Crumble barked.

Custard was already sniffing at a long fish, covered with thin green things. He took a big bite as Crumble climbed up onto the table.

"Yum – and yuck!" Custard spluttered. "The fish is nice, but that green stuff's horrible!"

"That's cucumber," Crumble said, taking a big bite himself. "Oliver puts it in sandwiches sometimes."

Custard turned to the other big plate. There was a big square of something meaty on it. "Mmm, this smells good!" he yapped. He took a lick. "Yes, it really *is* yummy!" he snuffled. This time he took a big bite.

Crumble, who had eaten half the fish by now, trotted over to have a taste, leaving muddy pawprints on the white tablecloth. "Oh, that's great!" he woofed when he tasted the meaty stuff. His tail wagged so hard, he knocked a basket of toast triangles off the table.

Custard went over to a bowl of

thick green liquid, licking the butter dish on the way. "Look at this," he woofed. "What do you think it is?"

"It looks like the cream Mrs Gill had on her face!" Crumble yapped back.

Custard wasn't so keen on tasting it after that. So he ate one of the crispy things next to it instead. "Help!" he barked. "It's hot!" He wiped his mouth on the tablecloth, trying to get rid of the taste.

Meanwhile, Yasmin was helping Oliver in the kitchen. She was washing lettuce whilst Oliver put the chicken drumsticks in the oven.

"Crumble and Custard are great," she sighed. "I wish I could have a puppy for my birthday. But I can't because of Dad's allergy."

"It's a shame," Oliver agreed. "I love Crumble and Custard to bits, even though they're naughty!"

He went over to the other end of the kitchen to get a saucepan. Then he stopped and stared at the big dish of crumble and jug of custard on the table.

"Yasmin," he said, puzzled, "I thought you put my crumble and custard in the dining room?"

"I *did*—" Yasmin began. Then her face fell. "Oh NO!"

Chapter Five

"I thought you meant the puppies!" Yasmin groaned.

She and Oliver rushed out of the kitchen. "I didn't know you meant the *pudding*!"

"I was so busy, I didn't even notice the pups had gone!" Oliver muttered. "Let's hope they haven't done *too* much damage . . ."

He opened the dining room door.

It was even worse than Oliver could have imagined. All the food was ruined. There were pawprints all over the tablecloth, and food had spilled on the floor. Crumble was just finishing off the fish. He had one cucumber slice stuck to his nose, and another on top of his head. Custard had decided to try the green stuff after all. His face was covered in it, just like Mrs Gill's facepack.

"My salmon! My pâté! My avocado dip and tortilla chips!" Oliver groaned.

"Hello," Crumble and Custard barked brightly. "We're just

finishing our lunch . . ." But their barks died away when they saw the look on Oliver's face.

"You bad, bad boys!" Oliver said. He sounded *very* stern. "Look what you've done!"

Crumble and Custard's ears flattened against their heads. They crept into the middle of the table and huddled there together, trying to make themselves as small as possible. They hated it when Oliver got angry.

"You've really done it now." Oliver was so cross, he could hardly speak. "*Look* at all this mess!"

"What's going on?" Mrs Gill appeared in the doorway, wearing a smart black dress. She gasped as she stared round at the room.

Crumble and Custard whimpered unhappily, and tried to hide behind each other.

"It was my fault, Mum," Yasmin said quickly. "I put the puppies in here."

Mrs Gill looked at Crumble with his cucumber slices and Custard all covered in avocado dip. Then to everyone's relief, she smiled. "Nothing's going right today," she laughed.

Then Yasmin had an idea. "Hey! We could get Oliver to cook the rest of my party food," she said. "I don't mind. We can always buy more tomorrow. And we've still got Oliver's lovely pudding!"

"Oh, why not?" said Mrs Gill. "And I'll take our guests into the garden – we won't be able to eat in here." She hurried out again.

Oliver glared at Crumble and Custard. "That's the last time you ever come to work with me," he snapped. Then he rushed back to the kitchen.

Yasmin picked up a napkin and wiped the puppies' faces.

"We're sorry, Yasmin," they whimpered sadly.

Yasmin gave them a hug. "Never mind," she whispered. "Come on, let's help Oliver."

Oliver was rushing round the kitchen pulling things out of the fridge and the cupboards. "Chicken drumsticks, mini pizzas, hot dogs, crisps, sausage rolls, burgers," he muttered. "I don't think any of the guests will be expecting food like this!"

"Mmm, I like burgers," Crumble growled to Custard.

"I think we've had enough to eat," yapped Custard.

They both sat quietly under the kitchen table.

Mrs Gill opened the kitchen door. "Everyone's asking when lunch is going to be ready," she said.

"In about half an hour," Oliver said, putting a tray of mini pizzas in the oven. "Can you keep the guests happy until then?"

"Oh, I think so," said Mrs Gill, spotting the crisps and cheesy puffs that Yasmin had tipped into big bowls. "Come and pass those around, Yasmin," she said.

Then Mrs Gill spotted Crumble and Custard under the table. She smiled. "Come on, you two," she said, scooping them up. "You're going to entertain our guests until lunch is ready!"

"Er . . . that might not be such a good idea . . ." Oliver began.

"Yes, it is," Mrs Gill said firmly. "They're so cute, they'll take everyone's mind off their rumbling tummies!"

Oliver looked sternly at Crumble and Custard. "Well, you two just behave yourselves from now on," he warned them.

"We will," the two pups barked as they went out into the garden with Mrs Gill and Yasmin.

*

The garden seemed to be full of people.

Mr Gill was running around arranging chairs and tables so that everyone could sit down.

"We thought we'd eat out here as it's such a nice day," he was saying brightly.

"I'm really looking forward to lunch," said a posh woman, who was wearing lots of gold jewellery.

"We will be eating in about half an hour," Mrs Gill announced calmly as she crossed the lawn, a puppy under each arm.

"Oh, I say, how cute!" exclaimed another woman, staring at Crumble and Custard. "They're not yours, are they?"

"No – *a-tishoo!*" said Mr Gill.

"They belong to our chef," Mrs Gill said. She put Crumble and Custard down on the grass.

The two pups really cheered up as everyone started ooh-ing and aah-ing, and saying how gorgeous they were.

"But I'm more gorgeous than *you*!" Crumble bit his brother's ear playfully.

"Ooh, no, you're not!" Custard protested, and attacked him.

They rolled over and over on the grass, pretending to fight. And then they ran round in circles trying to catch their tails until they were dizzy. Everyone laughed and applauded, except

for Mr Gill, who was too busy
sneezing.

Half an hour later, when Oliver
carried out trays of mini pizzas
and burgers, he could hardly
believe his eyes.

A well-dressed woman and two
men in *very* smart suits were on
their hands and knees on the
grass playing with Crumble and

Custard. Everyone else was watching and laughing.

"Crumble and Custard are a big hit," Yasmin said as she hurried to meet Oliver. "No one's mentioned food at all!"

Oliver smiled. "Maybe we'll get away with it," he said.

Crumble and Custard wagged their tails. Their owner wasn't angry any more.

"Well, here goes," said Mrs Gill. She took a tray of burgers from Oliver. "The guests are going to get a bit of a shock when they see what's on the menu!"

Crumble and Custard watched as Mrs Gill and Oliver carried the trays of food over to the guests. Would they like the food – or not?

Chapter Six

"That's the best lunch I've been to in ages!"

"Super idea to have kids' party food, wasn't it?"

"Yes, enormous fun!"

"And the pudding was wonderful – best crumble and custard I've *ever* tasted!"

Mrs Gill closed the front door behind the last guest, and smiled. "*Well*!" she said. "It seems our lunch was a big success!"

"Good," Crumble barked with a yawn. He snuggled down in Oliver's arms.

"Great," Custard added sleepily, as he did the same in Yasmin's.

"*A-tishoo*!" sneezed Mr Gill. "And we've got that huge joint of beef in the freezer."

"*And* we'll have to buy some more food for my party," Yasmin grinned.

"Yes, I had to go and cook more mini pizzas, burgers, *and* hot dogs," Oliver said. "There are none at all left now. I don't think the guests had eaten food like that for ages!" He glanced at his watch. "I think it's time we were going . . ."

Oliver carried Crumble and Custard outside and tucked them snugly into the sidecar.

Yasmin leaned inside and gave each puppy one last kiss. "Goodbye," she whispered. "I really wish I could have a puppy like you."

"Bye, Yasmin," the pups yapped sadly, as Oliver drove them away. "We're going to miss you . . ."

"And then all the guests said we were really cute, and started playing with us," Crumble barked.

"And they forgot all about the

food," Custard added.

It was Monday afternoon, and the puppies were at Granny James's house. It was a sunny day, and they were out in the back garden with Lady.

"Did we tell you about Yasmin?" Crumble went on.

"She's our *best* friend," Custard woofed. "Except for Oliver, of course!"

The old spaniel yawned. "You've told me all this already. You've been going on about it all day!" And she padded off to have a snooze under the lilac tree.

"Do you think we'll ever see Yasmin again?" Crumble asked, as he and Custard ran around the garden chasing butterflies.

"I don't know." Custard snapped at a big, buzzing bee that flew right past his nose. "I hope so."

Just then Mrs James came to the back door. "Crumble! Custard!" she called. "I've got a surprise for you!"

"Oh, what?" Crumble barked, rushing towards her.

"I love surprises," panted Custard, who was right behind him.

"Is it a juicy bone?" Crumble woofed eagerly.

"Is it pancakes?" Custard asked.

But it wasn't either of those things.

"It's YASMIN!" Crumble and Custard barked loudly. They

could hardly believe their eyes.

Yasmin was in the sitting room with Granny James. She rushed straight over to the puppies, and picked them both up.

"What are *you* doing here?" the puppies yapped happily, covering her face with kisses.

"My school's just round the

corner from here," Yasmin said breathlessly. "Oliver says I can come and visit you whenever I like, and Mum says it's OK too!"

"Oh, that's brilliant!" Crumble barked, thrilled to bits. "That's even better than a juicy bone!"

"And it's even better than pancakes!" Custard agreed joyfully.